To Dance With Darcy

Abbey North

Published by Abbey North JAFF Books, 2022.

This is a work of fiction. Similarities to real people, places, or events are entirely coincidental.

TO DANCE WITH DARCY

First edition. December 9, 2022.

Copyright © 2022 Abbey North.

ISBN: 979-8215853450

Written by Abbey North.

Blurb

Fitzwilliam gives his opinion of Meryton and its Assembly ball to Bingley before having a chance to thoroughly study the attendees. A woman with fine eyes catches his attention, but she rebuffs his invitation to dance. Miss Elizabeth Bennet quotes his own thoughtless words back to him and seems to find amusement in causing him discomfort as she ensures all in attendance know his thoughts.

He should try to steer clear of her, but when she's at Netherfield to care for her sister, they unexpectedly find common ground. His opinion of her changes, and hers seems to soften. When Mr. Wickham targets her, he feels compelled to protect her, unaware of another conspiring against them, and that their biggest obstacle will be Fitzwilliam himself.

This takes place during the period of the Bingleys and Darcy visiting Netherfield before diverging near the timeline of the Netherfield ball.

While Abbey sometimes writes sensual JAFF, this is strictly SWEET.

Chapter One

Fitzwilliam eyed the assemblage with a disdainful eye and a jaded curl of his lips. The backwater Meryton Assembly ball was as dull as he'd expected and filled with the buffoonery of the locals parading around in their finest. It was rather like seeing a sheep in a superb waistcoat. It was still a sheep underneath, and he had no use for the attendees or the event.

"Have you tried the ratafia?" asked Bingley as he approached, holding out a second cup for Fitzwilliam.

Fitzwilliam took it with an air of ennui, having a small sip and nodding just once. It would pass muster. It was certainly no worse than the lemonade served at Almack's. "It is passably tolerable."

"There is the Darcy I know, always happy to see the good in everything." Bingley teased him with an openly innocent expression.

Fitzwilliam set aside the cup of punch as he surveyed the crowd once more in an obvious fashion. "I fail to see how I would find anything pleasing in this lot, Bingley, even if I were prone to your ridiculously cheerful disposition, or my thoughts were as vacuous as yours. I can discover nothing motivating about this insipid gathering."

Bingley simply patted him on the shoulder and chuckled, clearly taking no offense to Fitzwilliam's rejoinder. "I feared you would behave in just such a way when Caroline and Louisa insisted you must accompany us. I realize you are tired from travel, but judge the people by Meryton's standards, not London's."

Fitzwilliam looked at his friend. "I have not the faintest idea how to even begin to do such a thing."

Bingley shook his head, clearly still amused. Fitzwilliam disliked providing amusement for someone else at his expense, but he managed to tamp down the urge to display his irritation to Bingley.

It truly wasn't his friend's fault he had been pressured into accompanying them all to the Assembly ball just hours after his arrival at Netherfield. In fact, Bingley had tried to suggest tactfully to his two sisters that perhaps Fitzwilliam was too tired to socialize this evening. Not that Fitzwilliam imagined he would enjoy partaking of the company around him even if he were in the best frame of mind.

"There are some lovely young ladies here, including the ravishing Miss Jane Bennet."

Fitzwilliam picked out the blonde-haired woman in the crowd and gave a shrug. "She is certainly the standard of beauty by which the other women must compare themselves in this crowd. I suppose she is as passably tolerable as the ratafia."

Bingley frowned, looking unsettled for a moment. "Are you truly fascinated by her?"

For just a moment, Fitzwilliam thought about pretending he was, simply because he wanted to get a rise out of his friend. It seemed unkind, for clearly, Bingley had settled on his newest infatuation. That it would be as transient as always mattered not, for Fitzwilliam had no intention of stepping between his best friend and a young lady. Taking pity, he said, "She is lovely, but she is of no interest to me."

"There must be some woman who catches your eye?" Bingley waved his hand around to encompass the room. "There are more ladies than dance partners, and I am certain you would go great distance toward ingratiating yourself amongst the locals if you offer to dance with some of them."

"No doubt, that strategy would work if I cared to do so. There are only a few worthy of my attention in this crowd, and I arrived with all of you. I have no interest in making local connections, forming friendships, or courting a countrified lass who probably has no idea how to behave in a London drawing room."

Bingley's mouth gaped open for a moment, and then he shook his head. He still seemed mostly indulgent as he patted Fitzwilliam on the back again. "In that case, I shall leave you to stew in your own superiority, my friend. I have one dance left with Miss Bennet, and I am intent on claiming it."

"Far better you than me, for I would not dance with this lot for anything." Bingley didn't respond to his words, and Fitzwilliam watched him walk away, feeling a slight stirring of envy.

For Bingley, it was easy to fit in with new circumstances and new people. He was a natural extrovert, and people genuinely liked him upon short acquaintance. Bingley never seemed ill-at-ease or awkward about how to respond, and he clearly enjoyed meeting strangers, who never remained such for long. For Fitzwilliam, that was a chore even when they were his equals. The people at the Assembly ball of Meryton were most assuredly not his equals, and they weren't worth the bother.

He was growing impatient with his post against the wall, yet eager to avoid Miss Bingley and her obvious interest in dancing a second dance, a fate which Fitzwilliam planned to avoid. Partially, he just disliked dancing, but it was also because Miss Bingley was far too avid in her attention.

She had made it subtly clear she would be quite pleased to be courted by Fitzwilliam, but that would never happen. She was a lovely enough woman, but he felt no attraction to her. Even if he did, her family was but one generation removed from trade, and he could well imagine the fuss that would cause amongst his relatives. Lady Catherine would likely have apoplexy, and his Uncle Fitzwilliam would be just as displeased.

He moved away from his current perch, circulating through the room. As he did so, his gaze caught on a dark-haired woman. At first glance, he looked past her, but something about her drew his gaze again, and he studied her more closely.

She had an ornate hat complete with an ostrich feather, but underneath it, he could see she had rich brown curls that looked like they had been carefully arranged. They framed a face that wasn't particularly remarkable until she smiled and laughed at something her companion said. His gaze briefly darted to that woman, but he looked away just as quickly. She failed to hold his attention, unlike the first.

His gaze settled on her brown eyes, and he had to concede they were very fine indeed. She had a pleasingly rounded figure, though her modest yellow gown made it difficult to see many details. It was startling, like coming across a rose in a bed of sand, and he found his feet moving toward her before he could think better of it. He arrived to stand before them, unacknowledged for half a minute. It was getting uncomfortable before a man he vaguely remembered meeting earlier in the evening stepped near. "May I make introductions, Mr. Darcy?"

Fitzwilliam nodded to the man, recalling he was Sir Lucas. "Yes, I would be grateful."

The older, stouter man turned to the two girls, who had fallen silent. There seemed to be an air of expectation about them, and he had the uncanny feeling they were on the verge of giggling. For some reason, he thought they might be tittering at him, and it left him feeling more uncomfortable than ever, but he persevered. After all, Sir Lucas was about to make introductions, so what choice was there? It would be insufferably rude to walk away now.

"Miss Elizabeth Bennet, and my dear, Miss Charlotte Lucas, allow me to introduce Mr. Fitzwilliam Darcy. He is a guest of Mr. Charles Bingley, who is leasing Netherfield, as you know."

There could be a slightly ambiguous interpretation by the way Sir Lucas called Miss Charlotte his dear, but judging from the age gap, he assumed she must be his daughter rather than his wife. She was a plain girl, though her smile lent a certain sweetness to her expression. He greeted her first by kissing her glove, mainly because she was the closer one.

His true interest lay with Miss Elizabeth Bennet though. He turned to her, taking her hand. It felt slightly stiff in his as he brought her glove to his mouth and kissed the back of it lightly. He didn't miss the way she tugged away almost imperceptibly, and he frowned in some confusion. He wanted to ask her to dance, but it felt awkward with Miss Lucas and Sir Lucas standing nearby.

Perhaps Miss Lucas realized that, because she said, "Papa, you never told me about..." She trailed off as she walked toward her father, putting her arm through his and suddenly leading him away.

When it was just the two of them, Fitzwilliam took a small step closer. It allowed him to speak more quietly without violating any bounds of propriety. "You are Miss Bennet?" At her nod of confirmation, he said, "I believe my friend Bingley has extolled the virtues of your sister, Miss Jane Bennet."

A genuine smile crossed Miss Bennet's face. "She is a charming woman, and I have yet to see a man who did not appreciate that." She tilted her head slightly. "Why, even you seem to grasp her beauty, Mr. Darcy."

He shifted in his Hessians, uncertain of her meaning, but it left him feeling prickly and wary. "Yes, she is charming. I suspect her sister is as well."

"Which one?" asked Miss Bennet in a sweet tone. "There are four of us, and though I think we are quite diverse in appearance and personality, you would no doubt find us all insipid."

Something in her tone alerted him, along with the use of a word he himself had used recently. Attempting to move past his discomfort, he said, "Your local musicians seem rather skilled."

"Yes, which is quite remarkable for a backwater like Meryton." Her tone was still sweet, and there was nothing in her expression to betray anything besides interest, but he still possessed an uncanny certainty she was mocking him.

Unaccustomed to such treatment, he was confident he would not receive it from the daughter of a gentrified landowner, so he chalked it up to his imagination. "I would be pleased if you would honor me with a dance, Miss Bennet."

Her eyes widened, and by the way her mouth dropped open, she was obviously greatly shocked. "I thought I heard that you would never wish to dance with anyone here at the Assembly? We are all too plain and insipid to catch your attention, are we not, Mr. Darcy? Save for Jane, of course." Her tone bordered on too-sweet now, and something flashed in her brown eyes.

He couldn't determine if it was amusement, ire, or perhaps a strange mix of the two. He cleared his throat. "Er..."

"I thank you for the charitable offer, but I find it unnecessary. Goodness knows, I could never compare to the draw of London, so I would not expect you to humble yourself to dance with me. It is certainly a miracle I have managed not to embarrass myself here at the Assembly ball at Meryton, and I could scarcely imagine how ill I would perform in a London drawing room."

He groaned softly, no longer doubting she'd overheard his imprudent words to Bingley. "Miss Bennet, I..."

Her lips pursed. "If you are going to apologize, there is no need, Mr. Darcy."

He breathed a sigh of relief, about to explain he was tired from his journey and out of sorts as it were, and that society and socializing held little appeal.

"I am certain it would be an insincere gesture, and I have no need for such artifice. If you shall excuse me, Charlotte appears to be trying to catch my attention." With a brisk nod, she turned and walked away from him.

Fitzwilliam stared after her for a moment, flummoxed by her behavior. None of the gently bred ladies in his social circle would have dared call him out on his comments even in such a subtle fashion. For a moment, he was offended that she had done so, and he rightly assured himself he had been correct in his judgment of all of Meryton.

As he turned and walked away, deciding he'd had enough of the Assembly ball and would spend the rest of the evening waiting in the carriage for his party, he found it oddly impossible to stop thinking of Miss Elizabeth Bennet. She had fine eyes and pert words, and she clearly had little use for him.

That was strange new territory for Fitzwilliam, who was used to being adored by both mothers and daughters of the *Ton*. It shouldn't matter to him what her opinion of him was, but it was unsettling that someone of socially inferior standing found him beneath her. He endeavored to set her out of his mind, but he had little success.

When Bingley, his sisters, and Mr. Hurst finally returned to the carriage more than an hour later, Fitzwilliam feigned sleep in a bid to avoid discussion. With his eyes closed, it was far too easy to see Miss Elizabeth Bennet in his mind's eye, and though he should probably forget all about her, he was certain he wouldn't be able to. He didn't know if he wanted to change her opinion of him, or if he wanted to give her a set down equal to what she deserved.

Chapter Two

Lizzy drew much amusement from Mr. Darcy over the next few days, ensuring everyone at the Assembly ball and all of Meryton heard his opinion of them. There was more offense than amusement in the reaction of her friends and neighbors, which Lizzy found mildly entertaining as well.

As she pointed out to Aunt Philips one morning after walking to Meryton on an errand for Mrs. Hill, what did his opinion of them matter? Mr. Fitzwilliam Darcy might consider himself better than all the people at Meryton, but his opinion mattered not in the scheme of things. In fact, she would consider any of her friends and neighbors of finer quality than him, for none of them would have been so rude as to share such a boorish opinion where anyone might hear.

She had to concede he must not have realized she was behind him though. Perhaps that would have tempered his tongue, but Lizzy wasn't convinced of that. He seemed like the insufferable, arrogant sort, and he likely would have blasted his opinion of all and sundry to anyone in the vicinity without a second thought.

Having done her best to so industriously spread the word of his opinion of Meryton and all the women, save Jane, it was with some discomfort that she found herself sitting across the table from him at Netherfield several days later. Her poor sister Jane was upstairs, having fallen ill the day before when she came to Netherfield to have tea with Miss Bingley and Mrs. Hurst. Mama's machinations had forced her poor dear sister to take the plow horse rather than the carriage, leading to being caught in the rain and exposed to the elements, which ensured her sister caught a nasty head cold.

Lizzy, worrying about her sister being surrounded by the Bingleys and Mr. Darcy, save for Mr. Charles Bingley, who seemed a decent chap, had hastened to cover the three miles between Longbourn and Netherfield on foot. She had arrived that morning complete with muddy petticoats which had clearly earned the disdain of Miss Bingley. Lizzy had shrugged it off then and did so again now as she took her napkin off the table and laid it on her lap. A footman approached with a taurine of soup, and Lizzy nodded her acceptance, inhaling deeply. It smelled like potato and leak, which was one of her favorite combinations.

"You must tell us, how is dear Miss Jane?" asked Bingley, his gaze earnest.

"Her fever is still high, but Mr. Jones left a few treatments for her. The apothecary believes she will be well enough to move back to Longbourn in the next few days." Lizzy winced at that, hating the idea of being trapped in this place for both herself and her sister, though clearly Jane had made a much better impression with the Bingley party.

"That is most unfortunate," said Bingley, looking truly concerned.

"Indeed, completely unfortunate," said Miss Bingley. "I suppose you will wish to stay with her?" The tone was perfectly polite, but the question and the expression were anything but.

Lizzy supposed the polite answer would have been to say if it were convenient, but she just nodded. "I cannot in good conscience leave her here."

"Of course not. Besides, you would be frittering away an opportunity to get better acquainted with us," said Mrs. Hurst with a tight smile. Her words sounded ostensibly friendly, but there was little doubt she was insinuating Lizzy was trying to worm her way into their favor.

She nearly snorted at the thought. The last thing she wished was to become bosom buddies with Miss Bingley and Mrs. Hurst. They were just the sort she'd always disliked—judgmental, condescending, and cold as well. "With any luck, our confinement here will end shortly."

She gave them a tight smile and spent most of the rest of lunch focusing on her food and only contributing when someone spoke to her. That was normally Mr. Bingley, who seemed oblivious to the tension around the table. Lizzy blessed him for being an innocent and naïve young man, but she couldn't help wondering a little about his intellect, or at least his ability to read people. He seemed to think everyone was satisfied with the situation.

"You will relay my regards to Miss Jane, Miss Bennet?" asked Mr. Bingley toward the end of the meal.

"I will as soon as she wakes again." Lizzy was antsy to escape this party, and she planned to stop by the library to procure a few books to keep her entertained while she waited for Jane's fever to break, and for her sister to be more interactive. It was with some relief that she left her chair a few minutes later when the party broke up, and she lingered just long enough to ask Mr. Bingley, "If you do not mind, I would like to avail myself of your library."

"Of course not. I confess, I have not read the books inside it, for I prefer to live my own adventures rather than read about others.'"

Lizzy frowned slightly. "I can say living your own adventures is quite exciting and necessary, but think how much you can learn and expand your horizons by reading? There are experiences you will never have. You cannot live enough lifetimes to have them all."

He shrugged his shoulders, looking unbothered by that. "You sound quite like Fitzwilliam." He touched his friend on the shoulder for a moment. "Did you not mention you were going to the library this afternoon as well, Darcy?"

If Lizzy hadn't been facing the prospect of time alone with Mr. Darcy, she might've been amused by his trapped expression. "I shall leave you to it then and procure books later."

"It is quite a large enough library for both of us," said Mr. Darcy with a hint of gruffness. "I will show you where it is." As he spoke, he stepped closer and held out his arm.

Knowing it would be rude to refuse, she threaded her arm through his. Lizzy expected to have to endure the short walk to the library, so it was with some surprise to realize being this close to him left her head reeling and her heart racing.

It was a most peculiar reaction, and she was strangely fixated on the scent of him. He smelled like pine and peppermint, and it was a pleasing combination. When they reached the library some minutes later, she found herself inhaling once more in an effort to remember his aroma as she stepped back and parted from him.

Mr. Darcy had left the door to the library open for propriety's sake, so Lizzy felt no qualms about being in the room with him, particularly when he crossed to go to the other side to browse books there. She acquired a few volumes to keep her entertained, and she wasn't surprised when Miss Bingley suddenly appeared in the doorway shortly after she and Mr. Darcy had arrived.

"What a charming little room," said Miss Bingley with a false laugh. "It is modest in comparison to the Bingley library, but I suppose it will do." She seemed to be addressing the comment to both of them, though her gaze was mostly on Mr. Darcy as she ventured deeper into the room, choosing a shelf near him.

"I do not believe I have ever seen you in the Bingley library," said Mr. Darcy in a neutral voice.

Lizzy almost laughed at the cornered expression crossing Miss Bingley's face. "I usually read before bed," she said after a moment. "Do you not enjoy reading before bed, Mr. Darcy?"

Lizzy frowned, finding Miss Bingley's intimate tone upsetting for reasons she couldn't explain. Technically, the woman was breaking no rules of polite society, but her posture and the way she spoke suggested her thoughts had gone to somewhere besides reading when thinking about Mr. Darcy in bed.

Lizzy felt a sudden flush as the idea came to her as well, and she realized she was just as guilty as Miss Bingley of imagining Mr. Darcy in bed, but he wasn't holding a book. Rather, there was a sheet draped over his lap, and she could see his bare chest. Never mind that she'd never really seen a bare chest of any man, save for her father's once or twice while they were swimming when she was younger. Her imagination seemed to provide a stellar image of how it might look. She cleared her throat and looked away quickly, as though he could read her thoughts if he looked into her eyes.

"I never realized you were much of a reader," said Mr. Darcy once again to Miss Bingley.

She shrugged a shoulder. "I aim to be an accomplished lady, Mr. Darcy. I believe you have enumerated the many qualities a fine woman should have?"

In spite of herself, she lifted her head and looked at them again, intrigued. "What might those be, Miss Bingley?"

Miss Bingley turned to her with a smile, though it didn't reach her eyes. "Of course, she must be accomplished in all the modern languages, be an excellent dancer, play at least two instruments flawlessly, have skill and flair for drawing, and incomparable manners. She must be an asset to a man like Mr. Darcy in every way, and she can have no weakness of character that might expose him or his position to vulnerability."

"That is a monumental list, Mr. Darcy," said Lizzy in her too-sweet tone. He must have recognized the sarcasm in it, because his jaw clenched, and his shoulders stiffened. "I wonder if you have met more than a half-dozen women who might possibly meet your requirements?"

"They are not my requirements," said Mr. Darcy stiffly.

Miss Bingley laughed. "I must disagree, Mr. Darcy, for I have heard you say such things yourself. Why, whenever you praise Miss Georgiana, you mention she is the pinnacle of feminine perfection. I know many ladies who strive to reach such heights and will never do so." She sent Lizzy a meaningful look as she said that.

Lizzy didn't respond, other than to shrug a shoulder and turn away from them again. "It must be quite exhausting to live up to your standards, Mr. Darcy."

"They are indeed high," he agreed with a bite in his tone. "Few women could hope to meet them, I concede."

Lizzy rolled her eyes, safe to do so since neither of them could observe the motion. "It would take a dedicated woman to be interested enough to strive for it. I admire the poor thing's tenacity, though I question her lack of desire to live a life of her own. It would be arduous to be the pinnacle of feminine perfection at all times."

"You must be relieved that no one expects such a thing from you, Miss Bennet," said Caroline Bingley with a cutting laugh.

Lizzy didn't let it bother her. "I am immeasurably relieved." She beamed at Miss Bingley as she said that before gathering her books. "If you will excuse me, I have enough to keep me entertained." Without another word to them, she exited the library. She couldn't help grinning as she imagined Mr. Darcy feeling a bit like a trapped rat in the room with Miss Bingley, for she had picked up on some tension between them.

Miss Bingley seemed far more interested in Mr. Darcy than he did in her. If Miss Bingley hadn't been so unwelcoming and unpleasant, Lizzy would have felt a spark of empathy or at least sympathy for her obviously unrequited interest. As it was, she couldn't find it in herself to be that charitable for the likes of Miss Bingley.

She entertained herself with the image of Mr. Darcy climbing the shelves in the library to escape Miss Bingley's increasingly ardent attention, chuckling lightly to herself as she entered Jane's room. While she read throughout the afternoon, she enjoyed a laugh more than once at Mr. Darcy's expense.

"WILL YOU JOIN ME FOR some fresh air?" asked Miss Bingley the next night after dinner. They were all gathered in the drawing room, and Lizzy was enduring the socializing required. Mr. Bingley had insisted she join them, and she could scarcely refuse now that Jane was awake and aware. Jane herself had implored Lizzy to make a good impression and show the sisters were more than products of their mother's gauche behavior.

She was here for her sister's sake, but she'd anticipated being ignored as she read in the corner. When she had declined to play a round of whist, that had seemed to be the extent of the social gestures that might be extended toward her, so it was a surprise to have Miss Bingley invite her to take a turn on the patio. She was certain there was some intention of malice behind the invitation, but she could think of no good reason to refuse.

She placed a ribbon in her book and set it on the coffee table before getting to her feet. "Fresh air would be delightful." Lizzy truly meant that, for she liked to roam all over the grounds and be outside, though she could scarcely imagine Miss Bingley venturing forth from her home without a parasol to shield her perfectly pale complexion with nary a freckle to mar it.

For the sake of Miss Bingley's complexion, it was a good thing it was nighttime, and the moon was full enough to provide ample illumination for them as they stood side-by-side near the stone rail of the patio moments later. Lizzy didn't speak, certain Miss Bingley had something on her mind, but she had no desire to make it easier for the woman to express it. It was unlikely to be anything positive.

"I noticed you and Mr. Darcy were speaking quite a bit this afternoon over tea."

Lizzy nodded, making no further comment. She had been surprised to discover she and Mr. Darcy had favorite books in common, and they'd had a surprisingly pleasant conversation for nearly an hour this afternoon while discussing "Don Quixote."

"It is the most relaxed I have seen him since we came to Netherfield." She shook her head. "He is dreadfully uncomfortable here, you know?"

"Is he?" Lizzy didn't want to invite confidence, because she was certain Miss Bingley had an angle, and it wasn't that she wanted to be friends.

"Yes, for everyone here is so dreadfully beneath us... Him. Do you know the illustrious lineage of the Darcy family?"

"I can honestly say, I have not given it a second thought," she said in a breezy fashion that made Miss Bingley's eyes widen.

"Indeed, you have not? I suppose that makes sense, for you would have realized on your own..." She trailed off delicately.

Lizzy wished she weren't so curious, for she would have ignored the bait. Yet, she couldn't help wondering what had compelled Miss Bingley to lure her out here. "I would have realized what, Miss Bingley?" She decided to cut to the heart of the matter.

"Why, you would have realized he is far too above your station, Miss Bennet, and you surely would have understood he is simply socializing with you because of etiquette. There is nothing more to it than that, and I would not wish for you to read more into it. You will only end up with your heart broken if you develop a *tendre* for Mr. Darcy."

"You speak of one who has experience in such matters," said Lizzy with a hint of sharpness. "Yet I must disagree with you."

Miss Bingley looked shocked. "You do not think he is above you?"

"Oh, I suppose he is socially and financially, but I have no special regard for Mr. Darcy. I do not care what his views are, or his opinion of me, as I have no interest in obtaining or holding his interest, Miss Bingley. I appreciate you being so kind as to be concerned about the state of my heart, but I assure you, I would never be so foolish as to waste it on someone like Mr. Darcy. I am not one for lost causes."

Miss Bingley looked almost constipated, as though she couldn't tell whether she should be happy, relieved, or irritated with Lizzy's words. "Allow me to clarify. You believe *you* are too good for *Mr. Darcy*?"

Lizzy frowned, though she wanted to chortle at the intense outrage in Miss Bingley's tone. "It is not a matter of superiority or inferiority, but rather of incompatibility. Mr. Darcy seems a rather stiff and rigid individual, and his standards are painfully high and exacting. I have no wish to try to meet them. It is as simple as that."

For another long second, Miss Bingley looked like a fish out of water, as her mouth opened and closed. Finally, she seemed to regain her composure and cleared her throat. "In that case, I have done my duty and warned you not to get invested in Mr. Darcy. I would not like to see you heartbroken."

"Do not be so coy, Miss Bingley. I am certain it would give you great happiness." With those less-than-polite words, Lizzy turned away from Miss Bingley and walked back into the sitting room, resuming her seat on the settee, and placing her book on her lap.

She looked up just once when Mr. Darcy made a sound of irritation while the nib on his quill snapped. As Miss Bingley bustled forward, offering to sharpen it for him, his gaze met hers, and he looked brooding, irritated, and perhaps a little sad. It was a strange combination, and even stranger, it sent a pang through her chest for reasons she didn't want to explore, so she hastily looked away.

Chapter Three

Fitzwilliam was still stinging from Miss Bennet's assessment of him. He knew what his mother would have told him—eavesdroppers never heard anything nice about themselves, so he supposed it was his own fault for hearing her true opinion. It left him restless and unable to sleep though, and he walked downstairs holding the candelabra, intent on seeking comfort in the library.

Books would offer solace for the hurt he couldn't explain existing. Surely, he was not so enamored with Miss Bennet that her words could cut through him this sharply. He barely knew her, and he should have a low opinion of her. He wasn't one to change his opinion or reevaluate after he'd decided on something, so having labeled her an unsophisticated country mouse, that should have been the end of it. She most certainly should not be haunting his thoughts, and he shouldn't be upset that she had professed no interest in gaining his attention or meeting his standards.

When he entered the library, it took a moment to realize there was already a light there. Just as he did so, there was a soft gasp. He looked up as he was closing the door, his gaze locking with Miss Bennet's. She sat on the settee, her legs draped across the cushions. She'd clearly made herself comfortable to settle in to read. She looked startled, and there was a flush in her cheeks that was most becoming by candlelight.

"Mr. Darcy, I did not expect anyone to be up at this hour." She clenched her fingers around her book, and he could see her knuckles turning white from where he stood several feet away. "I did not wish to disturb Jane, and her room is dreadfully dim for reading, so I thought I would come down and read alone for a while. I will leave the library to you though."

"There is no need to rush off." Even as he said it, he knew it was a poor lapse of decorum. Good manners dictated he should have opened the door the moment he saw her, excused himself, and returned to his room. She'd had the library first, so she should have top priority to maintain it. Most assuredly, they should not be alone together after midnight in this room.

He expected her to insist or protest and leave anyway. He held his breath until she nodded, looking a little uncertain as she relaxed slightly. "Very well."

When she bent her head, there was clear determination in her posture, and he was certain she was concentrating far more on the book than she truly needed to. He wondered if that was a reaction to his proximity and presence, and while he wanted her to respond to him, he didn't want to make her uneasy.

Abandoning his mission of seeking to read for the rest of the evening, he squared his shoulders, summoned his courage, and crossed the room to sit in a wingback near her.

She sat up completely when he did so, swinging around so that her feet were on the floor. "Do you need something, Mr. Darcy?"

"I heard what you said to Miss Bingley earlier." He practically blurted out the words, and they were completely lacking in finesse.

She frowned, looking as though she might question or deny something, but then her shoulders sagged, and she sighed. "I imagine you must feel insulted, Mr. Darcy. I should not have spoken out of turn like that, and I suppose I have a greater appreciation now for your professed opinion of the women of Meryton and our meager entertainments."

In spite of himself and the worry gnawing at his stomach, he managed to curve one side of his lips into a small smile. "Yes, I am somewhat familiar with the imprudence of speaking out of turn. I wish to know, is that your true opinion of me? You find me arrogant and yet beneath you?"

She shifted, looking uncomfortable. "Should I answer politely, or would you like the truth?"

His eyes widened at the choice, but he quickly said, "I would always prefer the truth from you, Miss Bennet."

"I do not think you are necessarily beneath me. In actuality, I wanted to give Miss Bingley a set down, for she was warning me away from you under the guises of friendship and concern. Yet it is obvious she holds only enmity toward me, so perhaps I reacted badly in an attempt to wound her. It was not my intention to wound you as well, Mr. Darcy. My first impression of you was one of haughty prejudice, but over the last few days, I have seen a different side of you. You are not nearly as intolerable as I expected."

His lips twitched slightly. "I fear I do not know how to respond to such exuberant praise."

That startled a laugh from her. "Oh, dear. I am insulting you once more. It was my intention to repair the damage I had done earlier, not extend it. "

He breathed a shaky side. "So, you truly do not find me odious?"

She frowned. "I do not believe I ever quite used that word, though perhaps with my friend, Charlotte." She had the grace to blush. "I do not find you intolerable, Mr. Darcy. I quite admire your sharp wit and understanding of literature, and you seem like a doting older brother. I imagine you must be a kind master to your servants, and there are likely countless people among the *Ton* who consider themselves lucky to be your friend."

"Would you be among them, Miss Bennet?"

She blinked. "I would hardly flatter myself to consider us friends, Mr. Darcy. There are too many differences between us, I fear."

"I would like to think that would not prevent us from forming a friendship, Miss Bennet."

She shrugged a shoulder. "I shall not be here for long."

"You will be here long enough for me to care about your opinion. I assure you, I value it greatly, Miss Bennet."

She seemed startled by that, and she pursed her lips for a moment. "That is surprising to hear, Mr. Darcy. In that case, I suggest perhaps we should both set aside our prejudices and try to become friends again. Or should I say, friends for the first time?"

"I would like that very much, Miss Bennet." The grandfather clock chimed one o'clock then, and he was startled by it. "Goodness, the hour grows late. We must not be caught in here alone."

Miss Bennet nodded as she stood up. "It would be disastrous for both of us to be compromised in such a fashion. You could hardly wish for someone like me as a wife, and I have no interest in a husband."

"I would like to think I would make a good husband." He wasn't certain what compelled him to defend himself, but he couldn't deny a surge of pleasure at the idea of Miss Bennet being his wife.

What a strange, unsettling thought to have at all. Her family would be a true burden, particularly her mother. He'd only seen her twice between the Assembly ball and a visit Netherfield to check on Jane the day before, but his impression was not good. He couldn't imagine he would ever revise his opinion and find Fanny Bennet acceptable in any fashion.

"Perhaps you would make a fine husband, Mr. Darcy. You would most certainly be a luxuriant one, but I am a woman of simple tastes. I much prefer my books and a quiet life to one spent in London or trying to please a husband. I have little interest in giving up what limited independence I am allowed under our laws. It would take a special man indeed to convince me otherwise."

"You do not believe I could be that special?" Why must he keep torturing himself with these questions? Did he truly want confirmation that she had no interest in him proving himself to her? Why he even felt the need to do so was still a foreign concept, and he should have ended this conversation long ago, even before it began.

She stared at him with unwavering intensity for a moment. "I think perhaps you could be, but that is not an avenue either of us wish to explore, is it, Mr. Darcy?"

There was a hint of hesitation and uncertainty in her tone, as though she wasn't even sure what answer she wanted. He was unable to still the compulsion to move forward, not stopping until only a few inches separated them. "Is it not?"

"Most assuredly not," said Lizzy. Despite the finality of her words, there was a hint of longing in her tone, and her eyes widened. Her nostrils flared, and there was a softness about her, an open vulnerability he couldn't ignore.

"Definitely not." As he spoke, he bent his head, brushing his lips against hers. It was a light, tentative kiss, barely more than a brief collision of his lips with hers before he pulled back. "I am thankful we have that straightened out, Miss Bennet."

She licked her lips, her gaze on his mouth as she nodded slowly. "Yes, it is better to know where we stand."

Unable to hide a twitch of his lips, he bent his head. "I shall leave first, so we are not seen departing together. When you walk by my room, please lightly tap on my door just once so I know you made it safely to your room."

She frowned. "How would I know which room is yours, Mr. Darcy?"

He felt a new surge of confidence as he slanted her a knowing look. "I have a feeling you might figure it out if you do not already know." By the becoming way she blushed, it was obvious she knew which room was his, though she wasn't going to admit that. "Good night, Miss Bennet." He murmured the words softly as he stepped back, retrieving the candelabra he'd left on the table and departing the library without a book to read.

Fitzwilliam went straight upstairs to his room, hovering near the door for several long minutes until he heard a faint, tentative knock. It was just the one, and for a moment, he pressed his hand to the wood, tempted to open the door and pull her into his room. He'd never had such a scandalous thought in his life, and only imagining her reacting with fear rather than curiosity and excitement held him in check.

He waited another few minutes, certain she must have returned to the room she'd been assigned in Netherfield by now before turning away from the door. Certain frustrations manifested in his anatomy, making it more uncomfortable to sleep than he would like, but he no longer wished to read himself into a state of slumber. Instead, he let his thoughts wander from one flight of fancy to the next, all featuring Lizzy Bennet in various mundane ways that somehow managed to make him fall asleep with a smile that he still wore when he woke the next morning.

Chapter Four

Lizzy and Jane had returned to Longbourn a couple of days ago, and while Jane was mostly on the mend, she was returning to the apothecary to fetch a refill of her sister's cough medicine. Mr. Jones would likely be in, and it seemed to make a true difference for her sister. Jane was still pale and coughing, but she would soon be ready to resume normal social activities.

Lizzy had expected to be relieved to go back to Longbourn, so it was somewhat unsettling to find herself out of sorts. She had returned home with the expectation of fitting in like usual, finding all the normal patterns of her life and embracing them, but everything felt just slightly askew now, as though someone had moved the world two centimeters to the left while she wasn't looking.

She hesitated to examine why that might be, and she absolutely refused to consider the idea that she missed Mr. Darcy, but she was blatantly keeping her eyes open for him as she walked into Meryton. She hadn't seen him since their departure from Netherfield two days ago, and she had no reason to expect to do so. The ball Mr. Bingley had promised Lydia he would host was happening soon, but that was still in the future, and she longed to have an excuse to see him now. It was silliness on her part, but she couldn't deny she wished to spend more time with Mr. Darcy.

They had spent quite a bit of time together her last two days at Netherfield, either in the library or walking the grounds, and though there had been no more stolen kisses, and their interactions had been perfectly polite and friendly on the surface, Lizzy was certain she wasn't imagining the undercurrents of awareness that flared and flowed between them.

She was still thinking about that as she stopped by Aunt Philips for tea after retrieving a new remedy from Mr. Jones for Jane's cough. She was unsurprised to see her aunt was entertaining soldiers, since Aunt Philips liked to be busy and have a lively social life. She and Lydia, along with Kitty, were quite enjoying the brief stay of the garrison of militia soldiers posted in Meryton.

For Lizzy's part, she was wary, for her younger sisters were inclined to impulsive behavior that might damage either of their reputations, and no soldier could afford to take a wife. Perhaps one with a captaincy or above, but the men her sisters had chosen as friends were of the lower sort, the kind who couldn't afford to marry or make a legitimate match, so Lizzy fretted after them.

Both her sisters could be terrible flirts and carelessly indiscreet, though neither of them meant any harm, and she was certain even though they were somewhat lax in that department, they wouldn't compromise their morals. Just the mere suggestion of them doing so would be enough to ruin either of them, and all their unmarried sisters along with them though.

Lizzy accepted a cup of tea, finding herself seated beside Mr. George Wickham. His attention was split between Aunt Philips and Lydia, who had ventured into Meryton sometime after Lizzy. Lizzy almost asked why her younger sister hadn't walked with her to the apothecary before coming to Aunt Philips's home, but she knew the answer.

She had warned Lydia and Kitty more than once to be on their guard and watch their reputations when interacting with the soldiers. Likely, she would have expected either another lecture or at least Lizzy's strong disapproval, so she had simply waited until Lizzy left before departing.

Mr. Wickham seemed like an affable fellow, though Lizzy didn't have much chance to interact with him until shortly after Lydia revealed where she had spent most of the last week. He turned to her then. "You were trapped in Netherfield with Mr. Darcy?" At her cautious nod, he said, "Mr. Fitzwilliam Darcy, correct?"

Lizzy was intrigued in spite of herself, and she nodded again as she sipped from her teacup. "I was. My sister fell ill, and it did not feel right to leave her there alone."

"That was likely a wise move on your part. It would be unsafe for her to be alone in a house with Mr. Darcy." He blushed then, looking away. "Pardon me. I should not have said such a thing."

Lizzy frowned, hackles rising in a defensive way. She struggled to dismiss the reaction and take a deep breath. "I do not know what you mean, Mr. Wickham, but I would appreciate enlightenment."

He looked around for a moment, as though gauging whether others were listening. He shifted slightly, leaning toward her so his voice was low enough not to carry, but he still maintained proper distance. "I should not speak out of turn, particularly about my betters."

"I assure you, I am not concerned about such a thing, so if you know something about Mr. Darcy, I would like to hear it." In contrast to her words, which sounded reassuring and open, Lizzy found herself grasping her cup too tightly. She had to focus on letting go and gently set it on the table lest she risk breaking the china.

"You see, Mr. Darcy and I go back quite a ways. We grew up together."

Lizzy couldn't hide her shock at the thought. How had a man who'd grown up beside Mr. Darcy ended up as nothing more than a lowly soldier in the militia? She was too polite to ask, but her expression must have betrayed her.

He gave her a slightly bitter smile, though it didn't seem like it was directed toward her. "Mr. Darcy's father was exceedingly fond of me. He left me a bequeath to become the next vicar of Kympton, but Mr. Darcy was jealous of the closeness between us, and he refused to honor his father's plans for me. He denied me a living and sent me away, partially because I had seen what kind of scoundrel he was."

Lizzy's eyes widened at the allegation. "Pardon me? I can scarcely imagine Mr. Darcy behaving like a blackguard." He seemed too stiff and proper for such shenanigans.

Mr. Wickham appeared chastened for a moment. "I would not wish to tarnish your opinion of him then, Miss Bennet." He sipped his tea as he looked down.

His dejection, coupled with his clear belief that she would rather maintain a good opinion than know the truth, prompted her to say, "I would prefer the truth always, Mr. Wickham."

With a sigh, and one more glance around, he said, "We were together at Oxford, for his father wished my education to be extensive enough to provide good spiritual counsel to the people of Kympton."

At Lizzy's nod of understanding, he said, "We shared quarters, and during that time, I saw Mr. Darcy behave abominably with the serving women and women of common origin. He favored the dance halls and gaming hells, but he ruined many a young girl outside those dens of inequity as well. They were all beneath his social circle, so no one cared or paid attention, except me."

"No." She gasped softly.

His face spasmed then. "Once, I mentioned to him that perhaps he should not behave so ungentlemanly with women who had no standing, and he assured me that if I did not mind my business, he would punish me. In the end, he did so anyway even after I avoided the subject." Mr. Wickham blinked rapidly, as though fighting back tears. "In his latter days, the elder Mr. Darcy was confined to bed, and he would not even allow me in to say my goodbyes."

Lizzy gasped, shocked that Mr. Darcy could behave in such an unfeeling manner. "That is tragic, Mr. Wickham. No doubt, Mr. Darcy, the elder Mr. Darcy, I mean, knew your feelings for him."

Mr. Wickham gave her a shaky smile. "I console myself with that knowledge. It was sometimes uncomfortable to find myself the preferred son, though I was of no biological connection to Mr. George Darcy, but I now hold some joy in my heart knowing at least one of his sons loved him, respected him, and treated him well. Mr. Darcy can be a cold, unfeeling man to everyone in his life, and his poor father was no exception."

Lizzy was disquieted, but she had little trouble believing it after she'd seen his chilly and haughty behavior firsthand. Yet, it contrasted with the impression she had gained of the man over the last few days. She left Aunt Philips' house sometime later feeling confused and torn about whether she wanted to believe Mr. Wickham.

Of course, it all came down to the truth, not what she preferred to believe. Which version was the real Mr. Darcy? Was he the supercilious man she had first met, the one who Mr. Wickham's account supported him being, or was he something different? Was he intelligent, indulgent, and more flexible than he seemed? She was no closer to knowing an answer, and Lizzy realized if she genuinely wanted to sort it out, she would have to speak with Mr. Darcy herself.

SHE HAD AN UNEXPECTED opportunity to do so a couple of days later when they received an invitation to tea. Lizzy was surprised to see it included her mother and all her sisters as well, and she imagined Miss Bingley and Mrs. Hurst had simply included them either for a laugh at her family's expense, or to please Mr. Bingley. Perhaps even at his behest, which seemed like the most likely explanation.

Whatever the reason, it allowed her entrée into Netherfield again before the ball, and she wasn't entirely surprised to see Mr. Darcy in attendance at tea. The event was composed of somewhat stifled and awkward conversation, though Kitty and Lydia managed to carry most of it as they chattered excitedly about the forthcoming Netherfield ball. Lizzy was quiet, often shooting contemplative looks at Mr. Darcy. Whenever he caught her looking at him, he would send a questioning look in return, and she would quickly look away.

Her strange behavior must have prompted him to want to speak with her, because after they had finished tea, he stood up. "I fancy a brisk walk around the estate. Would anyone like to join me?"

A cowardly part of Lizzy wanted to decline the vague offer, to pretend she had no questions, and perhaps to avoid learning the truth. She couldn't explain why it mattered so much to her to know the true nature of the man, but she suspected it was cowardice on her part that led her to avoid probing.

Disliking such a tendency, she stood up. "I shall join you."

"Walking is always good for the constitution," said Mr. Bingley as he turned to Jane. "Would you join us, Miss Bennet?"

"I would be delighted, Mr. Bingley." Jane had a slight cough, but she waved off any concern when Mr. Bingley expressed it. "No, I am fine. Mr. Jones told me some exercise would be good for expanding my lungs and restoring full function anyway."

Lizzy was somewhat surprised that Caroline Bingley didn't invite herself along, but perhaps she'd deemed Mr. Bingley and Miss Jane enough of a distraction to keep Lizzy and Mr. Darcy from spending too much time together. That was how she found herself walking beside Mr. Darcy several moments later, with Jane and Mr. Bingley a few steps ahead. There was enough distance to give some privacy to both couples, but not so much as to be considered improper.

"Something is troubling you." He spoke that as a statement of fact.

Lizzy's hand clenched reflexively around his arm where it rested in the crook of his elbow, and she cleared her throat. "It is not my place to bring up the subject, but..."

"Yes?" He arched a brow as he asked after the silence lengthened.

"I have met an old acquaintance of yours, Mr. Darcy. Do you know Mr. George Wickham?" As she asked, she carefully gauged his response.

Mr. Darcy's mouth tightened, and he looked angry for a moment. "The man is a scoundrel and a blackguard. You would be wise to steer clear of him to preserve your reputation."

She frowned, more confused than ever. "Would it surprise you to learn he gave me a similar warning about you, Mr. Darcy?"

He stumbled to a halt as he turned to look at her. "Frankly, it astounds me, madam, for he has no grounds to do so."

Feeling shy and a little embarrassed, Lizzy stammered out a repetition of the allegations Mr. Wickham had leveled against Mr. Darcy. She wasn't able to meet his gaze as she accused him by proxy of being a seducer and a despoiler of women.

He let out an angry hissing breath, and his arm dropped away from hers. At first, Lizzy thought he was distancing himself from her, but she realized it was just so he could pace around for a moment. His anger was obvious and seething, but his tone was more moderate than she expected when he turned back to her.

"Those are lies and twists of the truth, Miss Bennet. Mr. Wickham is offering you an account of his own actions while ascribing them to me. He was the one who corrupted more than a few young women during our time at Oxford. It was at that point I realized he would never be a proper shepherd for the spiritual wellbeing of the people of Kympton. Indeed, I would not trust him to oversee the spiritual wellbeing of a flock of geese."

In spite of the moment and the seriousness, Lizzy couldn't help a startled laugh at that. "Oh, my."

His expression betrayed no amusement. "I suppose he must have also told you I refused to give him the living my father had left him?"

She nodded, surprised he was mentioning that. "He did."

"What of the check?"

She shook her head, clueless to his meaning. "What check?"

He sighed impatiently. "I suppose it was an oversight that he didn't tell you I gave him a check for three thousand pounds to compensate after he refused the vicarage, though I would not have allowed him to have it if he had been willing. When he returned for more money less than a year later, I paid him again. It was only on his third attempt to squeeze another payment that I told him there would be no more."

Lizzy gasped softly, having a difficult time imagining the seemingly humble, modest soldier she had met yesterday squandering such a sum of money in a short amount of time, but there was something sincere about Mr. Darcy that made it difficult to disbelieve him. Mr. Wickham had seemed earnest as well though, and she was still confused.

"I thought I had seen the last of him until this past summer. My sister was in Ramsgate for a short time, wanting to assert her independence. You have not yet met Georgiana, but she is a sweet and naïve young woman, just now fifteen. Wickham saw an opportunity to ingratiate himself with her, and he convinced her they were in love. They were on the verge of eloping when I found out and stopped it. At the denial of receiving her dowry under any circumstances, Wickham disappeared, leaving poor Georgiana heartbroken. That is the kind of scoundrel Mr. Wickham is, and I implore you to guard your reputation around him."

Lizzy found it impossible to disbelieve Mr. Darcy now, for the pain in his eyes made it all too obvious he was telling her the truth. No honorable man would voluntarily tell a falsehood about his sister that might damage her reputation. That he was willing to tell her about the incident reinforced it must be the truth—and she was unexpectedly touched that he would share such a secret with her.

He also seemed to bear a load of guilt, as though it were his fault Georgiana had fallen to Mr. Wickham's predation. "It sounds as though you did everything you could to stop him."

"I did, but he never should have had that opportunity to start with. I had not been as involved in Georgiana's life as I should have, but that has since changed. In his twisted way, he brought us closer together, though his plan was to pull us apart and punish me while ensuring he had a large sum of my sister's money to waste."

Lizzy frowned. "I do not understand why he felt compelled to whisper all these lies to me. Why would my opinion of you matter?"

"Perhaps he wishes to turn everyone against me, and since he knew we are acquainted, he felt compelled to drip poison in your ear. Perhaps he realizes I desire more than friendship with you, Lizzy."

She gasped at the use of her first name, taking a step back. "How would he ever reach such a conclusion, Mr. Darcy?" She had barely begun to believe it herself, and she certainly hadn't said anything to anyone—not even Jane, who would never betray her anyway.

"Perhaps he has heard rumors, or maybe he is just intuitive. He was always good at reading people, and I am embarrassed to say he and I both have a similar type of woman to whom we might be attracted. You are definitely that type, so perhaps he inferred something just from your appearance. I do not know how his mind works, but I know he likes to twist everything and mangle it into something unrecognizable. I pray you will not hand him your heart to allow him to do the same to you."

She frowned. "I have no intention of giving Mr. Wickham anything, including the time of day."

"What of me, Lizzy? What will you give me?"

Lizzy was flustered and confused, uncertain of her own feelings, so she turned and started walking again. "We must catch up to Jane and Mr. Bingley. We are making poor chaperones indeed."

He issued an audible sigh as he started walking beside her, pointedly offering his arm. Part of her wanted to reject it, because she didn't want the temptation of being so close, but a bigger part of her wanted whatever contact she could get, so she curved her arm through his, and they started walking once more.

"Do you believe in love at first sight, Miss Bennet?"

It pained her that he was back to using her more formal surname, though it was certainly the most appropriate form of address between them. "I do not, at least not for myself." Even as she denied it, Lizzy felt a prickle of unease and perhaps a dart of guilt, as though she were fibbing to him.

"For yourself?"

"I believe it takes more time than an instant to love someone, though perhaps not for my dear sister, Jane. She is quite enamored with Mr. Bingley already, and she no doubt believes it is love. Perhaps it is, for she is rather uncomplicated, just like Mr. Bingley..." Lizzy trailed off as she realized Mr. Darcy had stiffened, and his expression was now closed. "Is something wrong?"

He cleared his throat, looking undecided for a moment. "I fear I must speak up. It is obvious to me that Miss Bennet does not hold strong regard for Bingley. Perhaps she is attracted to him, and he is most certainly enchanted with her, but from having observed their interactions, I am confident in saying your sister does not love Bingley."

Lizzy frowned at him. "I am just as confident in assuring you she does." Her words emerged in a starched tone, and she made no attempt to hide her irritation. "You do not even know Jane, save beyond a few basic interactions."

"Yet, I know her well enough to be certain she does not love Bingley. He deserves a true love match, not one prompted by a concern for material things."

Lizzy gasped and jerked back in shock. "What a dreadful thing to say, Mr. Darcy."

"When you came for tea at Netherfield recently, I overheard a conversation between your mother and sister, where Mrs. Bennet urged Miss Jane to do anything in her power to *capture* Mr. Bingley, and I quote."

Lizzy flushed, looking away. "My mother is rather uncouth, and she is overly concerned about such things as fortune and standing, particularly since there is no male heir, and Longbourn passes to a distant cousin via entailment after our father's death. However, Jane is not the same. She adores Mr. Bingley for himself, not for his fortune."

"She shows little evidence of that. She does not light up in his presence or treat him with any greater degree of warmth than anyone else."

She scowled up at him. "Jane is shy and reserved. Women are coached and trained to hide our emotions. We know men do not wish to be burdened with them, yet if we do not reveal them, then we are damned to be labeled gold-diggers? I cannot imagine being quite so cynical as you, Mr. Darcy."

"I am not cynical but practical. I saved my sister from a gold-digger, and I have no qualms doing the same when it comes to my dear friend. You should impart a warning to your sister to stop her pursuit before she breaks Bingley's heart."

Lizzy jerked away from him, suddenly unable to stand his touch though she had craved it moments before. "To do so would break Jane's heart. Your plan to divide them would break both of them, Mr. Darcy. I find you cruel and cold that you can imagine doing so this dispassionately."

"I am only thinking of my friend."

"And I am thinking of my sister and your friend." Without another word to him, Lizzy lifted her skirts, turned, and ran forward to catch up with her sister and Mr. Bingley. Jane was too captivated by Mr. Bingley to notice Lizzy's upset, to her relief.

She had no urge to turn around to see if he still walked behind them. She couldn't bear to look at him for another minute, and she refused to allow him to see the tears that started to slide down her cheeks. They were tears of anger, she quickly assured herself. After all, she didn't care enough about Mr. Darcy to shed any tears of sadness, loss, or pain on his behalf.

Chapter Five

Fitzwilliam was still upset at how things had gone with Miss Bennet, but what had been the alternative? He could scarcely allow Bingley to walk blindly into a trap set by a gold-digger, and nothing about Miss Jane's behavior suggested she truly loved his friend. Still, it pained him to have the separation between himself and Miss Bennet when they had been making progress.

As he walked into Meryton a few days later, having left Goliath behind to get new horseshoes, he found his thoughts returning once more to the confrontation between them. He couldn't help imagining how it would have gone if she'd given a different answer to his tentative question about love at first sight.

Fitzwilliam didn't consider himself a foolish romantic, and he'd never believed in such a concept before, but something had fundamentally altered inside him the moment he met Miss Bennet's gaze and saw her fine eyes across the Assembly room that night at the ball. Despite their arguments, disagreements, and counterviewpoints, he was convinced he could be happy with her. He'd been on the verge of declaring his intentions, fully expecting her to admit she believed in love at first sight. What woman did not, for wasn't it just the sort of soft sentiment tenderhearted creatures should treasure?

But not Lizzy. Rather than encourage him, she had distanced herself from him, and she was clearly still angry, for when he had gently insisted Mrs. Hurst invite Jane and Lizzy back for tea again yesterday, only Jane had arrived. That had been the absolute opposite of what he'd wanted, for it allowed her more time alone with Bingley, though Fitzwilliam had done his best to play chaperone and stay nearby, trying to thwart any attempts at closeness between the couple.

As he walked into Meryton, he admitted to himself this trip to town was simply an excuse to find Lizzy. He had done more walking the last couple of days than he had during all his time at Netherfield thus far combined, hoping to stumble across her either on the grounds of Longbourn or Netherfield.

There'd been no sight of her those times, but his heart skipped a beat when he saw her entering the tearoom ahead of him. He increased his pace, only drawing up short when he realized Wickham was following Miss Bennet. She seemed unaware of his attention or his presence, but there was a furtiveness in purpose and the way he moved that suggested he was deliberately following her inside Mrs. Fields's tearoom.

Fitzwilliam stepped forward, stopping Wickham's ability to do so. He grasped the man by the back of his collar and dragged him from the front door, which closed with a resounding *thunk* behind him.

Wickham turned, clearly ready for confrontation until he realized he was facing Fitzwilliam. Then he trembled slightly, and his posture changed. Likely, Wickham remained unaware, or perhaps was unable to resist, but he took on a demeanor of subservience as he stood facing Fitzwilliam despite his air of bravado. "I should not be surprised you have now sunk to dragging around others. What would your father think of your deplorable lapse of manners, Fitzwilliam?"

"He would think no less of me than he would you for being a vile scoundrel after the way you had behaved with Georgiana. You will stay away from Miss Bennet."

"I rather like Miss Bennet. She has a charming personality and a sympathetic ear. Of course, I could never take her as a bride, for her dowry is paltry at best, but she does not have to be a wife to bed." His expression contorted to become lascivious. "Was it not you who found me in bed with Miss White at Oxford, Fitzwilliam? Or was it Miss Greene? I can never recall."

"I believe her name was Miss Black, and she was but one of your many victims. Miss Bennet will not be one." As he spoke, he surged forward, grasping Wickham by the lapels. "I will destroy you before I allow you to touch a hair on her head or break her heart. I warned her way from you, and now I do the same to you. If you come within her vicinity, you will immediately take yourself away from it if you are smart. I would already like to destroy you for what you did to Georgiana. I will not allow you to ruin another woman. Do you understand me, Wickham?"

Wickham's jaw tightened. "What more could you take from me, Darcy? You have taken my living, banned me from my home, and denied me an opportunity to say a final goodbye to the man who loved me like a son... More than he ever loved you."

Fitzwilliam flinched at the words, though he knew they weren't true. That was the approach Wickham had always taken to try to undermine Fitzwilliam and leave him fully diminished, though he knew his father had loved him. "I did not deny you a final parting from my father. You were not at Pemberley, and I sent a message to you that he was fading. It is hardly my fault you did not arrive in time. By the time you got there, the physician was doing everything he could to save him, and neither of us were in the room when he passed."

"You will remember it however you wish, Fitzwilliam."

Fitzwilliam gave him a harsh laugh. "That is a rich accusation coming from one like you, Wickham. Steer clear of Miss Bennet and anyone else in Meryton, or I will see you stripped of your rank and deported to Australia."

Wickham's eyes widened. "I fail to see how you can do that. I have committed no crimes."

"I suspect you have left a trail of debts in your wake, just as you did at Lambton. I settled those, but I will certainly not be stepping in to settle anything more for you. It would be a simple matter to turn you over to debtors' prison. Watch yourself, Wickham."

With those words, he took a step back, waiting until Wickham had departed. He stood outside the tearoom until Miss Bennet finally emerged about a half-hour later. Her gaze fell on his, and she looked away from him as she passed. It was clear she had no intention of acknowledging him, though he could have tried forcing a confrontation.

He decided it was more prudent to give her space. When she calmed down, he would try to speak with her again. All she had to do was accept Jane's affection was far too tepid for Bingley, and their tentative attempts at a courtship could continue. He prayed she would have an epiphany sooner rather than later.

Chapter Six

Lizzy was startled to see Caroline Bingley walking across Longbourn land as she cut through a familiar path from Meryton that shortened her walking time considerably. Miss Bingley looked tired and slightly miserable, and though she had an enormous parasol, she was likely getting more sun than the redhead would like. Lizzy thought something might be wrong, so she approached cautiously. "Are you well, Miss Bingley? I do not often see you out walking about."

"I wanted to see you, Miss Bennet, but I did not wish to call formally at your home."

Lizzy's concern fled, and she stiffened her spine as she waited for Miss Bingley to catch up with her. She had no intention of walking any closer to the other woman, sensing this was going to be an ugly confrontation. "Why are you seeking me out, Miss Bingley?"

"I have come to warn you away from Mr. Darcy. I see how you shamelessly throw yourself at him, and I tried to be gentle with my previous warning, but it clearly did not sink in. You are not good enough for him, and should he deign to notice you in any fashion, it would simply end in a situation that was unsordid. He might make you a mistress, but he would never make you a wife."

Lizzy frowned, struggling to control her temper. "I would never sink so low as to let myself be any man's mistress, but you are wrong about Mr. Darcy and myself. I do not require your warning, and I thought I made that clear."

"I thought it was for a while too, but you are obviously interested in Mr. Darcy, and you continue to throw yourself at him. My words had no effect before, but I must tell you now that after whispers of your compromise, I cannot imagine Mr. Darcy would ever look at you again."

Lizzy opened her mouth to argue, but then Miss Bingley's words penetrated. "Compromise? What are you talking about?"

"It is all over Meryton that you have compromised yourself with a militia soldier. Someone named Wickham? It is said you meet privately with him at your aunt's house so you may indulge in all sorts of torrid actions. I am hardly surprised that someone of your standing thinks that is acceptable, but I would never allow you to taint Mr. Darcy's reputation with yours."

Lizzy was still reeling from her comments, so her words lacked heat. "It is hardly your place to step in, Miss Bingley."

Miss Bingley scowled. "I am concerned for a friend. Mr. Darcy might not be able to tell what kind of person you are, but I can. You want his money and have no regard for his reputation—or care for guarding your own."

Lizzy was shocked to be accused of being a gold-digger, just as Jane had been by Darcy, and she wondered what it was about the social circle of the Darcys and the Bingleys that led them to think they could accuse anyone beneath them of any perceived wrongdoing. She almost pitied them for constantly seeing machinations where none existed, based on the assumed desirability of their supposedly vaulted positions.

She glared at Miss Bingley. "You have said your piece, so now allow me to say mine. I have no interest in your opinion, your warnings, or your feigned concern on my behalf or his. It is not your business, Miss Bingley. Frankly, I am shocked at your behavior."

That had the desired effect of making Miss Bingley blush. "How someone of your nature could be shocked by my behavior is impossible to contemplate. Good day, Miss Bennet." With those cold words, she turned and walked away.

Lizzy turned away from her as well, in no mood to continue to interact with the other woman. Unfortunately, that lead her away from home, and she soon found herself back on the road to Meryton. She groaned low in her throat when she saw Mr. Darcy ahead. Short of darting away, there was no way to avoid interacting with him.

As he approached, she said, "I am rather glad I was not born in your social circle, Mr. Darcy. I would find it intolerable to think I am always a target because of my standing and wealth, or that I must impose my will on others and meddle where my input is not wanted."

His lips clamped. "Is this about your sister and Bingley?"

"No. Yes. Somewhat." She sighed heavily, realizing she was angrier than she'd allowed herself to feel before. It threatened to redirect toward him, so she took a deep breath, trying to calm herself. "Miss Bingley has just warned me away from you, suspecting I am a gold-digger."

Mr. Darcy looked shocked, which gratified Lizzy to a certain extent. "That is preposterous."

Lizzy allowed some of her anger to flow away. "I told her as much, and I advised her I did not have any care for her counsel or opinion. As though I would chase you for money." She allowed her disgust at the idea to show. "I am certain Miss Bingley's actions are prompted by jealousy, but I do not appreciate the allegations."

He looked uncomfortable, but he didn't deny her words. "I cannot believe she would imagine you are a gold-digger. You are far too honest and direct for such actions."

"As is Jane," said Lizzy with a hint of tartness, "Though I am sure you disagree."

"I am concerned for Bingley."

"And Miss Bingley is supposedly concerned for you, but I find it no less insulting that she would make such accusations."

He opened his mouth, but then it closed, and he looked unsettled. "I confess, I find it unsettling that she feels the need to speak on my behalf rather than leave it to my judgment."

A tingle of anticipation went through Lizzy as she realized that perhaps Fitzwilliam was on the cusp of an epiphany of his own. "You do not like it that someone else would presume to make your decisions in matters of your heart, Mr. Darcy?"

It was obvious he realized the paradox in which he found himself trapped. If he admitted he disliked Miss Bingley's intercession, then he would be forced to realize and acknowledge he had no place trying to interfere on Mr. Bingley's behalf either. If he didn't admit it, he would come across as a hypocrite, and Lizzy found that idea highly disappointing.

With a sigh, he nodded. "It was not Miss Bingley's place to speak on my behalf, nor was it mine to speak for Bingley."

"I understand what that admission must cost you. Yet you still believe Jane does not hold true affection for your friend. You are wrong, Mr. Darcy." She said the words without any irritation, hoping her utter conviction bled through instead.

His eyes widened slightly, and he took a step back. "Perhaps I have been too hasty in my assessment. I will reevaluate my opinion of your sister and the intensity of her affections. Regardless, even if I do not believe she loves Bingley the way she should, I will stop meddling, for it is not my place to do so."

"I am grateful you are willing to give Jane another chance for her sake and for Bingley's. I hope you reach the correct conclusion this time, Mr. Darcy. Do bear in mind that Jane is reserved and shy, and it takes time for her to warm up and reveal her true personality. I have no doubt she has shown that side to Mr. Bingley by now, but you will likely not be privy to it until you have known her for quite a long time."

He seemed to be truly considering her words, and he nodded. "I do believe I understand, Miss Bennet. I shall speak to Miss Bingley as well."

Lizzy held up her hand. "Do not bother. I have handled it, Mr. Darcy, and it does not matter anyway. She is imagining something that does not exist."

He surged forward, crossing the distance between them in under a second. His hand rested lightly on her shoulder, with his other cupping her hip. "Is she truly imagining it? Am I, Lizzy?"

How she wanted to deny his words, to pretend there was nothing between them, and she felt nothing for him. It would be the simplest thing in the world if she could just turn and walk away after assuring him it was all on his side and in his mind, but Lizzy was made of sterner stuff than that. "No, I suppose you are not."

He breathed a sigh of relief, and his head lowered for a moment. Lizzy lifted hers, fully expecting him to kiss her. Instead, he just brushed his lips against her forehead before taking a step back. She was disappointed and a little disgruntled at how he had returned to propriety.

"Will you reserve two dances for me at the ball, Miss Bennet?"

After a brief hesitation, she nodded. "I will, Mr. Darcy."

"Until then." He took her gloved hand, bringing it to his lips and brushing his mouth against the back before releasing her. Lizzy realized she was impatient for the arrival of the ball and to feel Mr. Darcy's arms around her, even in a casual quadrille.

Briefly, she wondered if they might play a waltz at the ball, and if so, would she have the nerve to prod Mr. Darcy to ask her to dance to it? It was still considered somewhat scandalous, particularly among the older generation, but she shivered with delight at the idea of dancing so closely with Mr. Darcy. What a strange turn of events, to find most of her anger toward him soothed, and to be anticipating what came next.

Chapter Seven

Lizzy looked around the ballroom for Mr. Darcy, finally catching sight of him shortly after their arrival. She tried to make it look casual as she worked her way toward him, and they happened to meet at the refreshment table. She didn't think she was imagining his strategic advancement as he worked his way toward her to meet in the middle.

She accepted the cup of ratafia he poured for her, finding it pleasantly fruity and enhanced with madeira. It was vastly better than the concoction they served at the Assembly ball in Meryton, and she reminded herself to be judicious with her consumption, for it likely packed a potent kick in spite of its mellowness.

"You look lovely this evening, Miss Bennet."

Lizzy smiled at the compliment, knowing she did look quite lovely in the white dress. At first glance, it was plain and perhaps even boring, but it made her skin luminescent and highlighted the darkness of her hair in contrast. White dresses were a dreadful chore to care for properly, so she rarely wore it, and he'd never seen her in it before. "You look quite dashing yourself, Mr. Darcy."

He fiddled with his cravat for a moment before dropping his hand to his side. "Has anyone claimed your dances yet, Miss Bennet?"

"I have barely arrived." She lightly wiggled the card hanging from the strap on her wrist. "Tell me, do you know if they will play a waltz this evening, Mr. Darcy?"

His eyes widened. "Are you allowed to waltz in Meryton?" The question was delivered with a hint of teasing.

"Perhaps it is frowned upon, but perhaps I do not care."

He grinned. "In that case, I shall make sure it is done. Allow me to speak with the musicians, and I will have a better idea of what dances to request."

Perhaps Lizzy should feel shameless, but all she felt was pleased. She beamed at him, accepting his withdrawal for a higher purpose. She watched him cross the room, standing near the edge of the small orchestra providing the music this evening. He was clearly waiting for a break, which meant they would be apart for a short time.

Lizzy allowed her gaze to stray, finding her sister and Mr. Bingley already on the dance floor. The way they pressed closely to each other for a moment was straining the bounds of propriety, but neither seemed aware. Jane was staring up at him, her lips parted slightly, and there was a becoming flush on her face. Mr. Bingley was looking down, clearly just as enraptured, and in that moment, there was clear and blinding love between them.

Lizzy was sure no one who looked at them could fail to see it, so she glanced at Fitzwilliam, pleased to find his gaze focused on his friend and her sister. When he looked at her, she gave him a knowing smile, trying not to be too smug, and he looked a little sheepish as he nodded just once. Perhaps he was satisfied with Jane's level of affection now. Even if he weren't, he'd given his word he would no longer interfere, and he would continue to maintain an open mind when it came to Jane. That was all she could ask.

"Miss Bennet?"

Lizzy stiffened and turned at the sound of her name, finding a young footman holding out a missive to her. She took it carefully. "This is for me?"

"Yes, Miss Bennet. I was told to find and give this to you."

Lizzy opened the letter after the footman had disappeared, surprised to see Mrs. Hurst was requesting an audience with her in the library. She had little doubt what Mrs. Hurst wanted to discuss, so part of her was tempted to tear up the note and ignore it, not wanting yet another warning to steer clear of Mr. Darcy.

On the other hand, she was tired of the Bingley sisters' meddling, so it was with some irritation that she set aside her cup of punch and departed the ballroom to find Louisa Hurst. She had every intention of telling the woman to mind her own business, but when she entered the library, she realized there was only a single candle burning. It seemed rather dim, and something made her nerves prickle with unease. Lizzy remained hovering in the doorway. "Mrs. Hurst, are you in here?"

"There is no Mrs. Hurst. Just me." The words were whispered softly, in a chilling tone. Lizzy turned to the left as Mr. Wickham emerged from the shadows, reaching for her. He tried to pull her into his arms, and she resisted, jerking back and slamming into the doorframe. It hurt her shoulder, but it kept him from closing the door behind her. At least she wasn't trapped in the room with him, but he pressed her body against the doorway, clearly intent on kissing her.

With a sound of disgust, Lizzy put her hands against his chest and pushed with all her strength. It was enough to make him stumble back a few inches, and she could have sobbed with relief when Miss Bingley appeared in the hallway. "What is going on here?"

"Please send for the village constable or Colonel Forster, Miss Bingley." Lizzy was trembling, and her voice sounded shaky.

Miss Bingley ignored her as she looked at Mr. Wickham. Conveniently enough, Miss Bingley was holding a candelabra that provided ample light. Lizzy's eyes narrowed as she said, "I always knew you would come to ruin, Miss Bennet." She sounded highly satisfied.

"I was ambushed. Your sister—" Lizzy reached for the envelope, but then she looked at Miss Bingley again. "Or perhaps *you* penned this letter in your sister's name, knowing I would not accept a meeting with you after the last one?"

Miss Bingley flinched, but she didn't confirm or deny. "Everyone will be horrified when they hear what I have discovered." She turned away then, clearly intent on returning to the ball. Lizzy reached out to grab her arm, but Wickham intercepted Lizzy before she could.

He jerked her back against him, and his breath was hot against her neck, making her queasy. "Why are you doing this, Mr. Wickham? You must know I have a small dowry at best. It is certainly nothing like Miss Georgiana Darcy's."

He stiffened for a moment at the mention of the other woman's name, but then he chuckled. "I do not need to be paid to ruin you, Miss Bennet. I have no intention of following through and taking the honorable option of marrying you. This is strictly to thwart Darcy. If it ruins your reputation in the process, I have little concern for that."

Lizzy was furious, and every second he held her was one second longer that Caroline Bingley had an advantage. If she reached the ballroom, she would blurt out what she'd seen, and that would be the end of her reputation. Prompted mostly by instinct, Lizzy slammed her heel against the toe of Mr. Wickham's boot.

He howled in pain as she winced too. Her thin slipper was no match for the stiff leather, but at least she'd had the benefit of knowing the pain was coming. She hobbled away as soon as he released her, breaking into an awkward run. Time seemed like it went too quickly, and surely, Miss Bingley was already announcing her disgrace to the assemblage, but Lizzy couldn't give up.

It was a reprieve when she got close enough to realize Mr. Darcy stood with Miss Bingley, but they hadn't yet entered the ballroom. She felt overwhelming relief, but then tension overtook her. What if he believed Miss Bingley's lies instead of her?

"I tell you, I saw them embracing, Mr. Darcy."

"I find that quite difficult to believe, Miss Bingley."

"It is somewhat true, Fitzwilliam," said Lizzy, boldly using his first name mostly to needle Caroline Bingley and imply there was a level of intimacy they had not quite reached yet. "It was all by design, of course."

She reached into her pocket and took out the letter that had ostensibly come from Louisa Hurst. "Do you recognize the handwriting?"

Fitzwilliam took it from her, opening the letter and reading for a moment as his eyes widened. "I do. I have seen this writing on letters to my sister Georgiana in the past. They were not from Mrs. Hurst though." He turned an accusing gaze on Caroline Bingley. "I recognize the hand that penned this indeed."

"I submit she and Wickham are working together to ruin me. Wickham admitted he had no intention of marrying me, and he did not care about my reputation being ruined. He simply wanted to hurt you and thwart any forming relationship between us, Fitzwilliam."

Caroline looked pale as Lizzy shared that information. She swayed and slumped against the wall. "It is not true, Fitzwilliam. Surely, you cannot believe these lies."

"I have little trouble believing them when the evidence is penned in your own hand, Miss Bingley. I will ask you to use my surname only, for we certainly are not close enough acquaintances for you to have leave to use my Christian name." His cold, starched words made the redhead flinch, but she didn't protest.

She bent her head and said, "I beg you not to tell my brother."

"I am afraid I cannot give you my word on that, Miss Bingley. Bingley needs to know what sort of company you are keeping, and what kind of actions you have tried to undertake in your bid to ruin an innocent woman and force a match between yourself and me. I assume that was your ultimate goal, was it not?"

Lizzy was glad for Miss Bingley's candelabra, which provided ample illumination to see the sick look cross her face. She wasn't proud of it, but she took some pleasure in seeing the other woman suffer, since Miss Bingley had so nearly brought about her ruin, along with that of her sisters. "I could not guarantee you would match with me, but I could not stand idly by and allow you to lower your standards to accept someone like her."

"Despite whatever the circumstances are of Miss Bennet's birth, and the inappropriate behavior of her mother, I find her a far more suitable match than I could ever find you, Miss Bingley."

Her eyes closed, and she seemed on the verge of collapse. "It is because our father was in trade."

Fitzwilliam quickly denied that, though she'd issued it as a statement of fact. "My relatives would be disapproving of that, and there was perhaps a time when I would have let such a thing bother me as well, but it has nothing to do with the matter. The truth is, I have no strong feelings for you, Miss Bingley, and I never shall. You are nothing but Bingley's sister to me, and that is all you will ever be. If you had succeeded in driving a wedge between myself and Miss Bennet, you would have been an enemy. As it is, you are not even a friend." He spoke almost gently, which was an even harsher contrast to the hard truths he uttered.

Miss Bingley didn't speak again as she turned away from them, departing from the hallway outside the ballroom and clearly intent on seeking solace somewhere else in Netherfield.

Lizzy hovered for a moment, eyeing Fitzwilliam uncertainly. "Do you have any doubts about the truth of the matter? I swear to you, I had no intention of meeting with Wickham."

"I believe you, and I also know he was not on the guest list. I made it clear to Mrs. Hurst and Miss Bingley both that he should not be invited." He grimaced. "No doubt, that was partially why Miss Bingley settled on the scheme, though she must have had Mr. Wickham's cooperation."

"Yes, I am certain she did. As I said, he was eager to help ruin whatever might be developing between us."

"For my part—" Before he could say anything else, the strains of the waltz started, and he held out his arm. "Shall we, if you still feel up to dancing?"

Lizzy nodded, putting her arm through his to allow him to lead her into the ballroom and onto the dance floor. She ignored the murmurs of shock around them, amused by how couples slowly trickled onto the floor to join them in the scandalous waltz. They didn't speak at first, just savoring the time with each other, and Lizzy was content to be in his arms. When the waltz faded, she was startled when a new one started, and her eyes widened. "Two waltzes in a row?"

His lips twitched. "It is shocking, is it not?" She giggled, and he pulled her closer. They were certainly straining the bounds of propriety now. "When you mentioned what was forming between us, I felt I must tell you something, Lizzy."

She tilted her head, feeling a hint of anxiety. "What is it, Fitzwilliam?"

"For me, it has already formed. I am deeply in love with you. I suspect I might have been from the first night I met you. From your fine eyes to your sharp tongue, there is nothing about you that I do not love. I will marry you via special license if you will accept, but I will settle for permission to court you and speak with your father."

Lizzy realized how fast this was happening, and how impetuous it would be to agree. It wasn't like her to make rash decisions, or to rush into anything without careful consideration. Taking a husband went against everything she considered important, but as she stared at him, she couldn't deny she loved him as well. "I love you, Fitzwilliam, and I happily ask you to speak with my father."

He seemed on the verge of kissing her, but they both managed to quell the reaction, knowing what kind of gossip would spread. He simply held her against him, and they basked in the moment. As the last bars of the waltz faded away, and the music for a quadrille began, he continued to hold her for a moment. "Will you dance with me again, Lizzy?"

Her eyes widened at the invitation. Three dances in a row was scandalous. It was practically declaring their engagement. It would set tongues wagging, and the gossipers would be delighted. She found she had little regard for them or for the talk it might inspire. The thought of pulling away from him was more than she could stand, and she arranged herself in position for the quadrille as she nodded. "I would be happy to dance with you, Mr. Darcy. Tonight, and for the rest of my life."

"I find myself unable to ask for anything else to achieve true happiness, Lizzy."

Epilogue

A few weeks later, Lizzy stood beside her new husband as they exited the church. Mr. Bingley and Jane followed right behind her, also having been joined in matrimony during a double ceremony. If Fitzwilliam had any doubts remaining about Jane's love and loyalty to Bingley, he hadn't expressed them, and Lizzy truly didn't think they existed.

He seemed open and welcoming with Jane, and he had heartily congratulated Bingley when they announced their engagement just a few days after he and Lizzy, though the official announcement had come from them a good two weeks after their scandalous third dance at the Netherfield ball, which had been followed by a fourth and fifth.

Lizzy doubted there had been any surprise at all among the folks of Meryton at their intention to wed. Only her father seemed caught off-guard, and he had bemoaned Mr. Darcy stealing her away. He'd even offered Lydia *and* Kitty and their dowries in replacement, though Lizzy thought he was probably joking. Maybe. Mr. Darcy had turned down that generous offer, insisting it had to be Lizzy or no one, while making it clear no one wasn't an option.

Lizzy's gaze sought out her father, who still looked red-eyed and a little tearful. She knew he was sad to be losing her, but she would ensure they saw each other as frequently as possible. Perhaps he could be persuaded to spend the summer at Pemberley. No doubt, once she got her mother on board with the idea—and that should be no struggle at all—Mr. Bennet would fall in line as well.

Looking forward to that, but not as eagerly as she was to her honeymoon, Lizzy joined Fitzwilliam in the carriage as Mr. Bingley and Jane took the opposite seat. There was a wedding breakfast to get through at Netherfield, and they would stay a few more days with the other newly married couple before embarking for Pemberley, but Fitzwilliam wanted to be there and settled before bad weather, and Lizzy was anxious to see her new home as well.

At least she'd already met Miss Georgiana, who had arrived before the wedding, and they seemed to be getting along well. Lizzy foresaw a few hiccups with settling in at Pemberley, but she anticipated finding true happiness there. After all, she'd already found it with Fitzwilliam, and with him beside her, how could she be anything else but happy regardless of her location?

PLEASE SIGN UP FOR Abbey's newsletter[1] to receive information about new releases. If you have any difficulties, email Abbey to request a manual add.

---

1. https://www.subscribepage.com/JAFF

About The Author

Abbey is a diehard Jane Austen fan and has loved Fitzwilliam since the first time she "met" him at age thirteen upon borrowing the book from the school library. He is the ideal man, though Abbey's husband is a close second. Abbey enjoys writing various steamy and sweet Jane Austen variations, but "Pride & Prejudice" (and Mr. Darcy) will always be her favorite.

Also by Abbey North

A Month To Love
Reproach (Part One)
Resentment (Part Two)
Rapport (Part Three)
A Month To Love Compilation

Classic Fusions
The Phantom Of Netherfield
Darcy's Christmas Carol

Crime & Courtship
Rapacity & Rancor: A Pride & Prejudice Variation
Abduction & Acrimony : A Pride & Prejudice Variation Mystery Romance
Extortion & Enmity: A Pride & Prejudice Variation Mystery Romance
Murder & Misjudgment: A Pride & Prejudice Variation Mystery Romance
Perfidy & Promises: A Pride & Prejudice Variation Mystery Romance
Crime & Courtship: A Sweet Pride & Prejudice Mystery Romance Compilation

Darcy's Courtesan
Adversity (Darcy's Courtesan, Part One)
Avidity (Darcy's Courtesan, Part Two)
Amity (Darcy's Courtesan, Part Three)
Darcy's Courtesan: A Sensual "Pride & Prejudice" Variation

Darcy Under the Mistletoe
Christmas At Pemberley: A Pride & Prejudice Variation
Darcys' First Christmastide
Mistletoe & Misunderstanding: Sweet "Pride & Prejudice" Variation

Marriage & Mysteries
Honeymoon & Hemlock

Mr. Darcy's Secret Stories
Mistaken Masquerade: A Pride & Prejudice Variation
Mischief & Matchmaking: A "Pride & Prejudice" Variation

Standalone
A Scandalous Proposition: A Pride & Prejudice Variation
A Bundle of Joy: A Sweet "Pride & Prejudice" Variation
Shadow of Darcy: A Sensual Pride & Prejudice Paranormal Variation
Darcy's Obsession
A Baby At Pemberley: A Sweet "Pride & Prejudice" Variation